Jazzy
and
Rhumbi

Special Thanks to
Louise Panelo, Kaye Parsons, Sid Wilson, Emman Villaran
and Ken Hoskin at Xlibris for all of their time and care.

Illustrated by Schenker De Leon.

To order additional copies of this book, contact:
Xlibris
844-714-8691
www.Xlibris.com
Orders@Xlibris.com

ISBN: Softcover   978-1-6698-7450-8
         Hardcover   978-1-6698-7451-5
         EBook   978-1-6698-7452-2
Library of Congress Control Number: 2023907402
Print information available on the last page

Rev. date: 04/19/2023

Jazzy and Rhumbi Adventures in MUSIC

DORI SEIDER

Ever since they were kittens, Jazzy and Rhumbi have loved music. All kinds of music thrilled them, and they would perk up their ears and reach to hear more. They became so attentive, and loved all the beats, the melodies, and the surprise sounds in places. Sometimes the music came from a musical instrument, like a piano, or it came from a phone, a TV, radio, or a person singing or humming.

When these active kittens became older and went to visit their relatives in Paris, their cousin Peggy entertained them with her recorder. Yes, they loved the food and pastries in Paris, but Peggy introduced them to music as well. That recorder music was such a treat and it even looked easy to play.

Music just affects these two felines. It makes them want to dance and sing.

Now, you may have already heard about these two cats, Jazzy and Rhumbi, who help their humans, The Noisy Guy and The Quiet One to rescue animals. They love to help in many different circumstances. When they were in Paris, they found a necklace and figured out how to return it to its rightful owner, Isabelle. So you will see later on in this book, how they will also come to use music to help others.

These two cats greatly admired a chef in a small Paris bistro (restaurant) who gave food to a family's dog, so they became inspired to become chefs and they invented imaginative recipes. You will find the recipes, with lots of ideas about good food, in the book *Jazzy and Rhumbi Become Chefs.* But let me tell you a bigger truth: these two cats love music even more than cooking and baking. They love music the most. In fact, when they cook and bake, they have music playing in the background.

As they have grown, Jazzy and Rhumbi have expanded their knowledge of different genres of music. This means different kinds, like classical, jazz, hip-hop, country, and many, many more. Some kinds of music, they have found, are so unusual that you can't even define them. You just have to listen and enjoy.

They take lots of music classes on their computers, studying for hours whenever they can, and they try to learn something new about music every day.

But here's the best news—they have started to create their own, original music! This makes them so happy, they can't even meow enough.

At first, our two cats appreciated watching and listening to Ronnie and Ani playing their flutes in front of a live group of friends and relatives. Now they also appreciate how many instruments can be played on their computer.

Jazzy and Rhumbi are intrigued to learn how to compose music on a computer. When they work on their computers to compose new music, it feels like magic! To create music, you play some keys on your keyboard, while your computer records them. So, in other words, you can create new music with a real piano keyboard or other instrument, like Ronnie and Ani with their flutes, or you can create new music right on your computer. Just like creating your own recipe to bake a cake and then offering some cake to your friends, you can create your own music and then share it with other cats or even humans.

Everyone seems to like a special kind or kinds of music, specific to them. There are always huge varieties of choices. And there is also silence. Silence is a form of music also. Sound makes music and soundlessness makes a different kind of music, the peaceful kind.

So Jazzy and Rhumbi were composing music one day, when their friend who is also a music lover, expressed a dilemma. "How can I raise the money I need to buy a keyboard that connects into my computer?" asked Eli, a small, short-haired kitten. Jazzy and Rhumbi could understand why Eli would want a keyboard, with all of its ways to express music—happy music, sad music, rhythmic music and all other variations.

Jazzy and Rhumbi both say at the same time: "Let's have a concert. We can invite guests at a reasonable price and then add it all up." So Jazzy and Rhumbi asked their friend Devin to play piano, and their friend Desmond to play guitar. Ronnie and Ani also said they could come and play flute. Ariana came to take turns playing piano with Devin. Matthew played the trombone.

Lyanna and Violet danced around the whole time. Toshaani listened intently, with a big smile on her face. Gianna and Jordan were having a blast. Tiara and her new kitten, Caprio loved being in the audience, which included a whole group of music-loving cats and dogs.

What a triumph! The music was fun, the guests were happy, lemonade and cake (yes, Jazzy and Rhumbi baked it) were served after the concert, and everyone asked if they could do this again some time. Enough money was raised to buy Eli a keyboard. And not only that, but several of the guests wanted to learn how to compose music on a computer, so Jazzy and Rhumbi gave them a preliminary introduction to how you can do this.

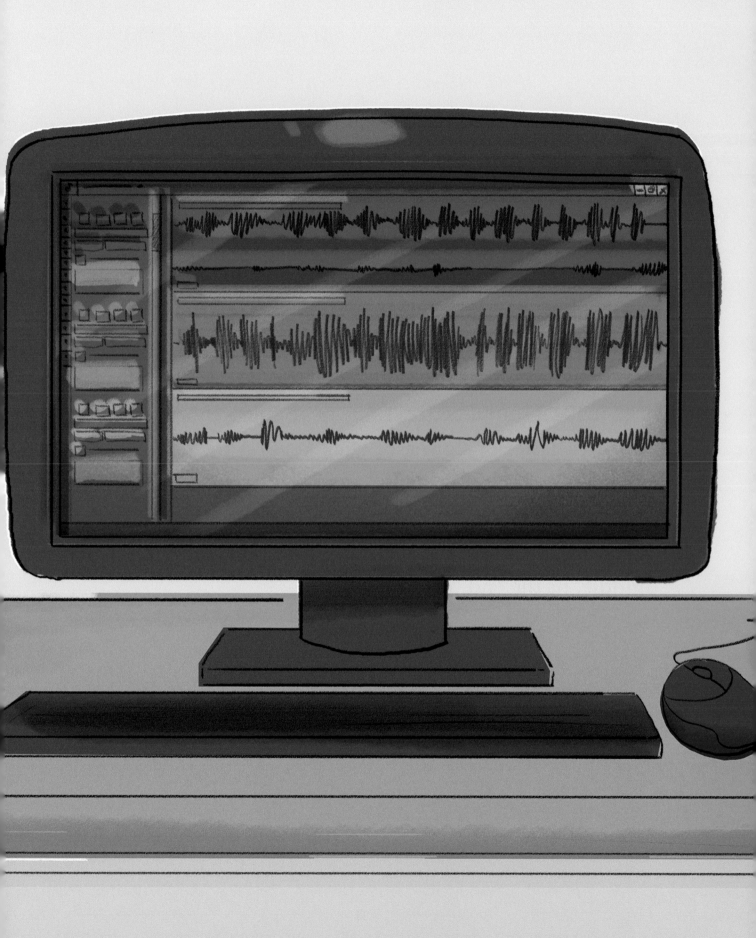

After you have recorded what you played on your keyboard, you will see it on the screen. When you see your music in small lines in your tracks, or in soundwaves in your tracks, you will then be able to *edit* your music. That means change it to make it sound better. You will be able to make it louder or softer, faster or slower, or click keys on the computer to change your music in many other ways. The biggest thing that Jazzy and Rhumbi found out, is that you can click on a region and move it to the beginning of your song, the middle, or the end.

The first time Jazzy and Rhumbi realized that they could actually **move music around** on their computer, they were grinning from ear to ear, giving each other PAW-5's, and jumping up and down. They were so happy and excited, that they ran to tell Noisy Guy and Quiet One : "You can move music on a computer."

Now what is all of this big fuss about moving music? Let's think about this for a minute. You already know, for example, that when you paint a picture, you can decide to have a tree on the left, the right, in the middle, or anywhere else you would like. You can color it in expected colors, like green and brown, or even in unusual colors, just for fun.

So why can't creating music be like doing a painting? You can have a group of sounds at the beginning, the middle or the end of a song. The music can be very much like music you have heard before, or it can be unusual music, like no one has heard before. If you can move music, you can also delete some notes, add others, and change it any way you want.

In other words, when you do a painting, you are the painter and you create original paintings, unique to you. When you compose music, you are the composer, and you create original music, also unique to you.

Jazzy and Rhumbi had already tried several things on their phones and computers, like wishing people happy birthday, taking photos and videos, and texting, but even so, they *still* were amazed by what you can do with music!

So they thought to themselves: *"What do you do when you want to learn more?"* And then they signed up for online classes, one right after another, to learn about music in general, and to learn about computers and music, specifically.

They learned things like: *"What is an ostinato?"*

Answer: A stubborn note that you repeat over and over. Have you ever been stubborn and just kept saying the same thing over and over? Well, an *ostinato* does the same thing— it gets stubborn and keeps repeating itself.

Jazzy and Rhumbi also learned how to compose relaxing music, with long, slow sounds. And they studied rhythmical music, with lots of drumbeats. They learned about hip-hop music, jazz music and many other genres.

They even took a class online about violin music with Itzhak Perlcat, who taught in his class that the sound of a violin could be smooth, like butterscotch. They loved the sounds that Itzhak Perlcat said could be made with a violin, like *pizzicato.* (At first they thought that was pizza for cats, but then they looked it up.)

Jazzy and Rhumbi felt so lucky when they found excellent teachers online. Their first teacher was Graham, who taught them the software program so that they could compose music intelligently. Graham made them want to continue on—he was so inspiring! Next came Michelle, who played guitar and sang beautifully. She encouraged them to add cello sounds to their piano music. Then came Jason, a wonderful teacher who explained everything so well. They took tons of classes with Jason. And finally, they were so enthusiastic they took many more online classes with Mikael, who taught them important musical concepts. He also taught them everything from slow, relaxing music to epic cinematic music, to scary music, to exciting, adventure music.

Jazzy and Rhumbi were in awe of their teachers and beyond grateful to them. How could any cat not appreciate the ones who helped them understand music, play music, listen to music, and remember to insert silence also? Jazzy and Rhumbi were now ready to devote a big chunk of their cat life to the art and science of music.

Jazzy and Rhumbi gave each other PAW- 5's for sticking with their classes and never giving up, even when it seemed just too difficult. They emailed their teachers to thank them for their devotion, without which they would have never learned so, so much. Deep gratitude is what Jazzy and Rhumbi felt.

And now our two musical cats can teach other cats to compose music with joy, and to listen with joy. Music is universal. This means it is for everyone, no matter what form of it you like.

After their practice session, all of the music artists sat around eating Jazzy and Rhumbi's home-baked banana bread and drinking Jazzy and Rhumbi's healthy berry smoothies. (For recipes, Jazzy and Rhumbi would love for you to read their book *Jazzy and Rhumbi Become Chefs*.)

They then became philosophical about music. This means that they talked about how music makes them feel, what you can use it for, what it means for each of them, and other stuff. The musicians agreed that when you are happy, music can make you even happier. When sad, it can cheer you up quickly or allow you to feel your sadness and slowly let it go. Music can also provide energy for your exercise routine.

Music serves all the purposes you can imagine. For Jazzy and Rhumbi, it is the very soul of life, and that is why they create it wholeheartedly.

When teaching a kitten how to compose, they say things like: "Think of rain and see if you can create sounds like it, either on your instrument or your computer instrument." Another thought exercise may be: "Think of another kitten going up and down the stairs. Try it slowly, and then quickly." A third exercise for their students is: "Think of a sound you like, any sound, and then see if you can create something like that sound on your instrument or on your computer instrument."

After you compose, Jazzy and Rhumbi wondered, where do you send your music to be finished or polished? (This used to be called mastering). As it turns out, a lifetime friend of theirs, Elliot the Cool Cat, does just that. He takes their music files and makes them sound even better.

Elliot the Cool Cat, asks himself whether the tracks Jazzy and Rhumbi send him are too loud or too soft, whether or not some sounds interfere with others, and what he needs to do to make the sounds fuller or richer. When he is done fixing up the sound of their tracks, he sends back an improved version of their original music. His own kitten, JoJo, an orange Tabby, plays while Elliot works.

Elliot can be called an *audio engineer,* but don't be scared away by the words. He really just fixes things up, while he listens over and over again, until it sounds great.

If you decide to create music yourself, because it is one of the most fun and also most fulfilling things in life, a very important thing to know is that you don't have to be perfect for your music to be great. It's O.K. to make mistakes, no one is perfect, and the more mistakes you make, the more you will learn. Don't be too hard on yourself.

Jazzy and Rhumbi know that when you play your instrument, you want your music to have the correct notes. You want *quality,* which means the music is very good. But how do you get that quality? By continuing on after you have made lots and lots of mistakes and have learned from them. You can learn thoroughly and consciously from each and every mistake you make, so that your mistakes become gifts of learning.

Jazzy says, "Hey Rhumbi, I want to learn more and more about music and never stop. Rhumbi says, "Me, too!" Jazzy says, "Just think, we can create music with pianos, harps, flutes, oboes, clarinets, violins, cellos, trombones, trumpets, French horns, drums, taiko drums, timpani drums, bells and so many other world instruments. And this is even before adding sound effects, like *reverb,* which makes the music *reverberate,* spreading sound around the room.

We can love music from all over the world, and as we continue to create music, new worlds of sound will open to us. "Hey! That's what music is to us, an adventure into endless possibilities." Then Jazzy and Rhumbi look up, and hanging in their living room is a painting by internationally renowned painter Joy Irven. They had seen her paintings on their trip to Paris and had bought one to take home. The name of the painting is *Endless Possibilities*.

"Endless Possibilities"
Joy Irven

Acrylic

To all of you who love music in any form, any time and anywhere in the world, we, Jazzy and Rhumbi know that it can bring you great comfort, and sometimes make you happier than you could ever imagine. Keep experiencing all of those endless possibilities, and thank you so, so much for joining us on our musical adventures.